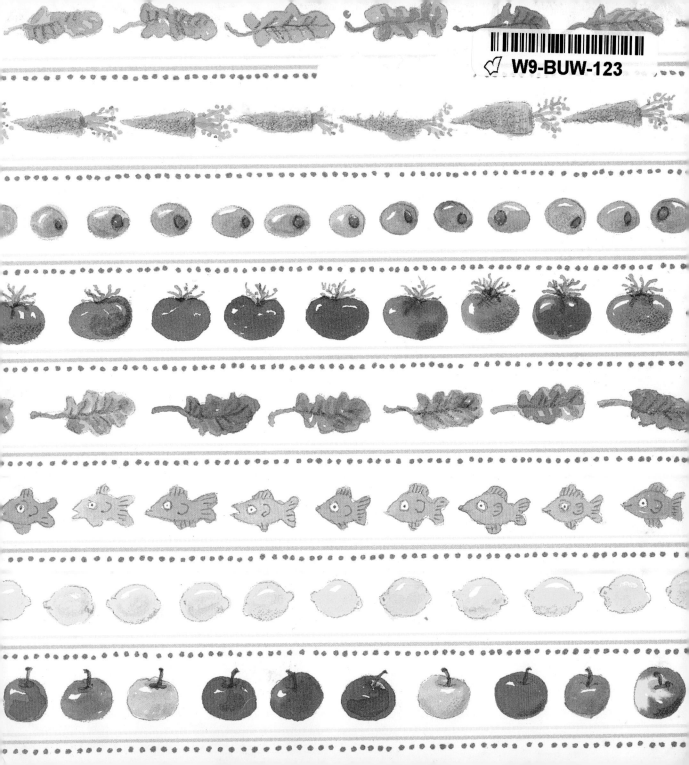

D.W. the Picky Eater

Marc Brown

Little, Brown and Company

Boston   New York   Toronto   London

For the least picky eater I know,
Laurie Krasny Brown

First Edition

Library of Congress Cataloging-in-Publication Data

Brown, Marc Tolon.
    D.W. the picky eater / Marc Brown. — 1st ed.
      p. cm.
    Summary: Because her eating habits cause some problems, Arthur the
aardvark's younger sister has to stay home when her family eats out.
    ISBN 0-316-10957-6
    [1. Food habits — Fiction. 2. Aardvark — Fiction.] I. Title.
PZ7.B81618Dwt   1995
[E] — dc20   94-25674

10 9 8 7 6 5

WOR

Published simultaneously in Canada by Little, Brown & Company (Canada) Limited
Printed in the United States of America

D.W. and her brother, Arthur, were helping Mother unpack the groceries. "Yuck!" said D.W. "I'm not going to eat this!"
"You've never even tried it," said Mother.
"It's looking at me," said D.W.

"I don't eat anything with eyes, or pickles, tomatoes, mushrooms, eggplant, pineapple, parsnips, and cauliflower. Well…and maybe a few other things. I would never eat liver in a million years, and more than anything else in the whole world, I hate spinach!"

"Face it," said Arthur. "You are a picky eater."

On Wednesday, Father surprised D.W. when he packed her
lunch for play group.
"Did you eat your sandwich?" he asked on the way home.
"It fell in the dirt," said D.W. "It was an accident."

Thursday at dinner, D.W. pretended to try the Hawaiian
Shrimp.
"I saw that," whispered Arthur.

Emily invited D.W. to stay for dinner on Friday.
"We're having spaghetti!" said Emily.
"May I have mine plain, please?" asked D.W. "No sauce."
"That's the best part!" said Emily.

"Are these little green things spinach?" D.W. asked when her spaghetti arrived.

"It's parsley," said Emily. "Try it."

While everyone else ate, D.W. just moved her food back and forth into little piles.

"You'll never be a Clean Plate Ranger at this rate," said Emily.

On Saturday, D.W. and her family went out to eat.
"This salad has spinach in it!" cried D.W.
"Just try it," said Mother.
"She's going to have a tantrum," warned Arthur.
"Please try it," said Father.

"No!" said D.W., and she pounded her fist onto the salad dish.

"I'm so embarrassed," said Mother.

"No more restaurants for you," scolded Father.

From then on, the family went out to dinner without D.W.
"I'd rather stay home with a sitter anyway," said D.W.
Mrs. Cross only allowed carrot sticks for snacks. And at
exactly eight o'clock she said, "Bedtime. Now march, quick
like a bunny!"

One morning at breakfast, Arthur twirled a tiny paper
umbrella.
"Where did you get that?" demanded D.W.
"At the Chinese restaurant," said Arthur. "It was fun!"
D.W. began to wonder what she was missing.

"Tomorrow is Grandma Thora's birthday," announced Mother. "Our big night out!"
"I want to go, too!" said D.W.
"You will have to eat what's on the menu," said Father.

"I will," said D.W.

"You will have to try new foods," said Mother.

"I will," said D.W.

"Even if it's green and looks like a leaf?" asked Arthur.

Everyone got dressed up Saturday night. D.W. wore her black
shoes with the bows, even though they pinched her toes.
"Happy Birthday, Grandma Thora!" said Arthur and D.W.
together.
"I hope they have plain spaghetti," prayed D.W.

D.W. was happy when she sat in her chair. "No one will see me if I have to get rid of something disgusting," she thought.

"I'm Richard," said the waiter. "Here's a kiddie seat for the little lady."

"Thanks a lot," said D.W.

"Do you have food with little umbrellas on it?" she asked.

"We do not," said the waiter.

Everyone ordered except D.W.
"You'd better bring her the kiddie menu," said Arthur.
Father read D.W. the menu.

◊Children's Menu◊

Three Little Pigs in Blankets

Farmer in the Deli Bagel Platter

Pirate Pita Pocket

Little Bo Peep Pot Pie

Goldilocks Griddle Cakes

Three Bears Burger and Fries

"Time to choose," he said.
"I guess I'll have the Little Bo Peep Pot Pie," said D.W.

When dinner was served, all eyes were on D.W.
She took a bite.
"This is good!" said D.W.
D.W. took another bite and another.
She drank all her milk.

"Good work!" said Mother and Father.
"I'm very proud of you," said Grandma Thora.
Arthur checked under the table. "Where'd you put it?"
he asked.

"I could eat this every night," said D.W. "Will you make it for me at home? Please?"
"I'll need the recipe," said Mother.

"What a good little eater," said the waiter when he cleared D.W.'s dishes.
"It was delicious," said D.W. "How do you make that?"
"Very simple really," said the waiter. "Just take some pie pastry and fill it with . . ."